I0631211

William Entriken Baily

Modern rhymes

William Entriken Baily

Modern rhymes

ISBN/EAN: 9783337271732

Printed in Europe, USA, Canada, Australia, Japan

Cover: Foto ©Andreas Hilbeck / pixelio.de

More available books at **www.hansebooks.com**

MODERN RHYMES.

MODERN RHYMES.

BY

WILLIAM ENTRIKEN BAILY.

"Some said, 'Will, print it;' others said, 'Not so.'
Some said, 'It might be good;' others said, 'No.'"

PHILADELPHIA:
PRINTED BY J. B. LIPPINCOTT & CO.
1879.

CONTENTS.

MODERN RHYMES.

THE TRIUMPH OF HOPE.

THERE dwelt in Arcady in olden days
A swain bred up in quaint, primeval ways,
Whose contentment forbade a wish to roam
Away from pleasures of pastoral home.
The changing seasons found his prudent hand
Ready to fertilize or reap the land;
To prune young trees, or aid each sprouting form
Withstand the beating of the sudden storm;
To gather ripened fruit of golden hue,
Which glanced between green leaves with pearly
    dew;

To guide numerous flocks upon the plain,
Where verdure urged their growth to eke his gain.
The neighb'ring husbandmen envied his state,
And strove his industry to imitate.

One eve he calmly walked a fragrant vale
To muse and Summer breezes to inhale,
Beneath great oaks (whose branches gnarled
    above
Their shelter served for the slumberous dove),
As multitudes of stars, each with chaste ray,
In parts enlightened his wandering way;—
When lo! there came a faun notes to breathe
    through
A pipe unique with assiduity true.
First mildest melody was made to flow,
Fascinated with Orphean pow'r slow;
Then such was heard to lull a god in pain,
Bid Sorrow dull to Lethe move amain.
Soon the faun ceased, issued from shadows drear,
Advanced towards the swain observant near,
Proclaimed a mission from Oberon great,
Who ruled the fairy realm in regal state;

And who, aware of debts to diligence blest,
The pipe upon the swain's acceptance prest.
The faun the movements then taught of strange
    sleight;
How to adroitly cause throbs of delight;
How to force, when wished, strains or loud or
    low,
Those more difficult which sweepingly flow.
This done, the gift received, with silent pace
He sought the mysterious haunt of his race.
   Oft thereafter the swain within a bow'r
Was wont to recline and breathe tunes an hour,
As in meridian splendor Sol was seen
To beautify the earth. On the grass green
Soon Phebe (idol of his ken) would stray,
A crook in hand, to hear his winsome play,
As little lambkins would about her rally,
Ceasing to woo or in the shadows dally.
From parts adjacent shepherds thronged in view,
Watched in silence new wonderments ensue.
Such facile pow'r deigned not to grace his skill
When each essayed the borrowed tube to thrill;

Again, with fervid tongues, the swain begged they
Apply his vigor transport to convey;
He, complying, bid clefs, moods, quavers greet,
Now   wild,   now   strange,   and   now   so   deftly
      sweet
That long the music lingered in the ear
As though poured down from some delicious
      sphere.

A proclamation made the swain one day
That either he or she as well could play
Upon the curious pipe should, for that tact,
Possess it e'ermore mankind to attract;
The judges to be two youths of high birth,
Famous in Arcadia's realm for truthful worth.
His confidence and pride had grown so great
He deemed his merits none could imitate.

To distant countries spread of this the news
As people gathered to strive or refuse.
In vain some impelled with pure vital air,
As the judges bid their trifling forbear;
Others, inexpert, caused harshness to prevail,
When gibes from auditors them to assail

Arose; but none with spontaneous art
Awoke the finer feelings of the heart.

In time, from a dominion unknown, came
Three maidens,—Mirth innocent; Pity tame,
With downcast eyes; Hope, fairest of the three,
Who moved like one conscious of majesty.

Their place of emulation was a mead
Where the grass-blade rose from the tender seed;
Where a small brook on sands appeared to stray,
Whose crystal murmurs never flowed away;
Where seductive groves, upon every hand,
Outstretched long limbs cool shadows to expand
O'er tiny solitudes. Between two trees,
On a knoll, sat the swain like king at ease,
Ready to employ a various store of tunes
That all competitors might know his boons;
The two gallant judges on either side,
Dressed in new garments, their especial pride;
Of high and low degree, encircling stood
People, waiting events in quietude.

After the swain had blown, to introduce
The rivalry, many graces abstruse,

The fair applicants were bidden draw nigh,
Each in her turn, harmonious forte to try.

  First Mirth the low knoll faced.   Her locks
     displayed,
When zephyrs mild with stealthy motions strayed,
The twinkling charms; and on her cheeks were
     spread
Blushes of health which swelled, then changed,
     then fled ;
Adorned the dress upon her figure neat
Gayest ribbons; and on her little feet
There were the rarest slippers ever borne,
Save those of yore by Cinderella worn.
She, with strange actions like a fickle fish,
Applied to pipe her lips fain to ravish,
Inspired excitement, stored the air with sound,
New joy appeared in faces ranged around.

  Pallid Pity came forward next to vie,
A melancholy aspect in her eye ;
Remindful, by a timid, abstract mien,
Of a haunting ghost in moonlight's empire
     keen.

A veil was on her head, a band around
Her virgin waist; a long skirt trailed the ground.
Whilst endeavoring attention to beguile
Commingling whispers were suppressed awhile.
She calmly inspired an emotive train,
So prone to sympathize with human pain;
Led by feats of harmony dolesome, slow,
To contemplate on misery cold and low.

Then Hope eagerly advanced with meek glad-
  ness,
Uninfluenced stood by preceding sadness:
Embraced a cincture rich her fragile waist,
Adorned with jewels, clear as crystal chaste;
A superb garment robed a figure fine;
Bedecked a golden chain a neck divine;
Upon her head there was a chaplet rare,
While white petals perfumed loose, wavy hair.
First she, with simple self-abandonment,
A measure, leaving its soul-soothing pent,
The rosy valley of her lips breathed through
Which gently diffused an enchantment new.

Anon she altered tones, commanded motion
Like easy winds that shift the waves of ocean.
They suggested a warrior to the view,
Who wore a helmet plumed, a keen sword drew,
Upheld a blazing shield, his soul aglow
To meet, on quivering battle plain, the foe.
Her subtle art rolled forth with varied force,
Gathering strength like river in its course;
Then louder, louder swelled to speak of fate,
And then of triumph, then of glory great,
As glad elation thrilled with mantling heat
And the heart moved quick in its rosy seat.

When she had forborne acclamations loud
Awoke far echoes; next the motley crowd,
Forestalling the judges, on her for aye
Bestowed the prize, with which in many a day
Forthcoming she might from Woe's forlorn train
Reclaim mortals. To crown her new-born reign,
They dowered her with wreaths of roses made
(Cultured by wood-nymphs in the mystic shade),
Whose virtuous perfumes diffused a power
To animate like a rainbow after a shower.

The swain, alack! with a reluctant will,
His pipe resigned; and oft, at noontide still
Thereafter, longed for it; but he no more
The tuneful fav'rite grasped 'neath bowery store
Himself to solace or shepherds to please,
Or lead sweet Phebe from a languid ease.

HOPE.

THE evening hour has come; there's silence
    on the lea;
A lonely shadow lurks beneath yon aged tree,
And timely sadness seems pervading in the air
To slowly paint it with the colors of despair.
Somehow anxious thoughts infest the dolorous
    mind;
They brood on things agone, to better themes
    are blind;
The moon high in glory escapes their dismal view,
They see cavern horrors or dripping dungeon dew.
A wandering lamb bleats upon a hillock nigh,
Crickets hidden attempt to sing, low breezes sigh;
But they beget, not check, weird Melancholy's
    dream,
Which sternly holds—avaunt ye dreadful things
    that teem!

Go to a rocky subterranean cell and dwell,

Where night's e'erlasting hours like Pluto's shades
repel!

Go rid me of yourselves! ye agonize my breast!

As long as ye delay as long am I from rest.

Turns the soul most weary; it yearns with passion strong

For purer sphere than this, and calls this world
a wrong,—

But lo! there comes a voice, it bids me wait
awhile;

'Tis nimble-witted Hope who lures us all with
guile.

I see her beauteous form, her lithe and gentle
motion,

Her lovely eyes so keen, as sparkling as the
ocean.

Go sadness! come gladness! I know not what
to do,—

The very stars above seem different to my view!

THE RIVER.

———

RIDING
In a boat which is gallant and free,
Down a river transparent to see,
Is the Monarch of Bliss, who is loud with his
        mirth;
    Guiding
With vim in his mien as a pilot of earth
        From Woeland to Wonderland away.

    Curling
Are currents of the stream to the right
And the left when islands are in sight;
Then they recklessly leap from large stones to
        the roar
    Whirling,
The dashes of bubbles and dew-balls before,
        From Woeland to Wonderland away.

Veering
With caution on tumults of the tide
Is the craft by hid dangers to glide,—
By breakers and bowlders and wrecks which are
rough,—
Steering,
As it passes to deeper expanses ungruff,
From Woeland to Wonderland away.

.

Flushing
Are rare gems in the bed of the stream
Amid glitter of tints that there teem;
And waters are quivering with fishes of gold,
Rushing
Like an arrow of speed from an archer of old
From Woeland to Wonderland away.

Skimming
Are green leaves with the odor of bowers,
And bits of blossoms and of flowers

In petal-like glory deliciously red;
     Swimming
(Perforced by movements to a mystery dread,)
     From Woeland to Wonderland away.

     Gleaming
Are thin rises of mists and their shreds,
That are robed in rich sunny-dyed threads
To enter the fanes of the Fades of the air,
     Teeming
In invisible realms under spiritual care
     From Woeland to Wonderland away.

     Springing
Is a bird to the welkin's vast sphere
To utter a keen carol to cheer,
As onward and onward the waters are borne,
     Singing
Near the banks of a meadow where roses adorn,
     From Woeland to Wonderland away.

Riding

In a boat which is gallant and free,

Down a river transparent to see,

Is the Monarch of Bliss, who is loud with his
mirth ;

Guiding

With vim in his mien as a pilot of earth
From Woeland to Wonderland away.

THE WONDERFUL VALE.

SUGGESTED BY OVID'S METAMORPHOSES.

Down in a green vale of ancient days when the
    story
Strange of the gods, miracles was often retold;
When the then mild month of June, endowed
    with her glory,
Scatter'd on high hills the dewy glances of
    gold;
    When murmured a river that ran
    (Oft reflecting the visage of Pan);
When the unseen birds in shades their music
    unrolled;—
    Were the happenings odd to narrate
Briskly in rhymed lines this Winter waning and
    late.

Trees are numerous, with trembling leaves on
    the sprays,
  Near to the stream's bank like a grove devoted
    to mirth ;
Narrow are way-paths to depths remote from
    the rays
  Shed from the blue sky to sparkle motes of
    the earth ;
    And profuse are flowers of smell
    That lowly and soberly dwell
(Porters of dew-pearls to boon to Noon at her
    birth);
    And the butterfly's sensitive glow
Flutters and journeys unsteady-like to and fro.

Wide in the East smooth is the landscape to a
    mountain,
  Whereon are shepherds aloft with pipes that
    are fain
Calmly to make soothing tones like purls of a
    fountain

Spreading at night-time on sable quiet their
    strain ;
  And the bleats are there heard of the sheep ;
  And the goats are oft shifting to leap
Down from the great rocks, where dangers rug-
    gedly reign,
  To where breezes of Summer serene
Move and incline low the grasses tinted with green.

Come from the deep grove the noisy hums of
    the tongue ;
  Yet are accents far; not audible to the ear
Words in distance said. Soon maidens merry
    and young
  With their persiflage and laughters loud will
    appear
  On this side of the bushes and shades :
  Now for a view of the beautiful maids !
Cracking on hard ground beneath are twigs that
    are scar
  As the music of fun is elate,—
Blue is the hue—see ! the nearest limbs agitate.

Gathers a gay throng of maids in fulness of sight;
 Sparkle the kind glances that preside in their
  eyes;
Flutter odored locks which bear the roses so
  bright
 Weaved into garlands to crown; on cheeks
  are the dyes
  Enamelled by Nature's own hand,
  That heighten when blushes expand;
Seen are the white teeth between the lips; and
  the vies
 Of the vein strive for purple that's pale.
Seem they like fish guileless which in oceans
  prevail.

Gracefully move they about with steps that are
  agile.
 Viewed are the pattering sandals upon the feet
Held by the laced thongs to ankles bare. Softly
  fragile,
 Twirling the timbrels, their fingers; neat and
  as fleet

Are their actions as motions of sleight
In illusions of magic to sight.
Blue is the cincture embracing loosely to meet
At the rear in a bow and to go
Freely at will down the kirtle skirt in a flow.

Circle they soon, hand-in-hand, an oak that is
near;
Sober then becomes their mien, more grave
what is saith;
Rise on the warm breezes tunes to float to the
sphere;
Louder the brief chorus; they next cease for
fresh breath;
Then sweeter and stronger they sing
With a swiftness no echoes can ring,
Hid in the rude grots afar, with mockery's
wealth;
Then revolve they about the large tree
Fleetly like a rim whirled around a cork on a
sea.

Lonely in bow'r complaining 'neath shades that
    are dreary
  Ah, is their Queen fair! recounts their sorrow
    in song;
Gone is her Love far to foreign realms, and are
    weary
  Thoughts in her vexed heart from morn till
    shadows do throng.
    They plead he may soon to a rest
    Return with a victorious crest,
Never to roam more from native land to prolong
  The encounters and dangers of war,
Chieftain of brave hosts who shield the arrows
    that pour.

Charmed are the shepherds with shreds of sound
    that are floating
  Far from the fair choir within the wonderful
    dell;
Ceasing to thrill pipes they turn to hear the de-
    noting
  Voices that render the solemn musical spell;

And they eagerly rise to their feet
As though new happiness to greet.
Startled to silence, the sheep untinkle a bell,
And with goats that are fearlessly high,
Gaze on the valley, the idol shrine of the eye.

Filled with a strange sense the swains remove to
the right;
Seek they the path formed up side of mount
·　from the plain
Down to the low grove to come.　With flocks
from the height
Stretch they in one long array, most zealous
to gain
The source of pleasure for the ear,
Their wonder to appease anear.
Winding by great crags, which threat to tumble,
the train
Descends to the bed of the vale;
Causing by movements thousands of grasses to
quail.

'Tween is the wide stream, but never daunted,
    all glide
Into it swimmingly swift (an action for sheep
Wontless) to reach banks before with muscular
    pride,
  Which, with fatigue, soon are safely gained, as
    the sweep
    Of the waters below is made roll
    Into depths that are filled like a bowl;
Then each, with form dripping, is most cautious
    to creep
  Nearer and nearer to the grove:
Muffled are murmurs that hummed like beeves
    in a drove.

Quietly all stand anon, with simple delight,
  Gazingly before the maids surrounding the tree,
Swelling their mild tones to plead a deity of might
    Grim in a huge trunk, and who unseemeth to be
      In the likeness of material wood,
      With a bark about him for a hood
Gnarled and remossed by the touches of a century.

Lo! a struggle of branches is heard;
Sounds, too, a hoarse voice that yearns to utter
some word.

Metamorphoses the tree to shape of a sage,
  Rough and giant-like, whose lofty breath in the
      air
Spreads from his mouth mists to curl in flight;
      and his age
  Seemeth to be old, for white are rolls of his
      hair
    (That were ere but the leaves on the top
    Of the oak); and his garments low drop
Foldingly round loins. A wand, slender and bare
    (On which the acorns were arrayed),
Calmly he shakes, whilst the distance hears in the
      shade:

"Maids of the vast earth, I come, but not to
      grant grace;
  Come I to change. Time, the god of life, hath
      a mould

Given me mystic to man, by which, and apace,
  Commuted are things to features new to be-
    hold."
    As quivers the ground of the vale
    He moves, and a sound of a wail
Heard is upborne.   Wafts his hand on high to
    unfold
  A power unseen to unroll
Maidens and swains, flocks in forms inert for
  the soul.

Then the fair Queen comes anon, still pensive
    her plight,
  Slowly the soft maids to seek who strayed
    from her bower.
Alas! with swains they've gone for ever from
    the sight,
  Changed to the trees decked with leaf and
    blossom and flower.
    She returns to her biding-place lone
    In silence to there utter low moan;

But to her ne'ermore was known their fate from
  the Power
  That reigned in the valley supreme,
Like a deity great of whom a fabler may dream.

THE HORSEMEN.

HARK! up the mountain from East at the morn,
  As the hemlocks are forbidding clear view,
Tones of the bugle from blowers are borne;
  Noises and neighs are commingled there, too.

See! in the Valley of Time are now riding
  Horsemen as though they were eager to gain
Brightest of goals where a Summer's presiding
  O'er an eternal devoid of heart pain.

As they issue from domains of the past,
  Various and brilliant, with easy delight
Beheld are castles alluring and vast,
  Such as the fancies reveal to the sight.

There, in the van, with a banner of beauty,
  Goeth the chieftain to lead the long way;
" Follow!" he cries, "ye great spirits with duty;
  Glory is ours ere the end of the day."

Then for a moment from bugles abound
  Musical thrills; and the neck of each steed
Quivers with ardor as lightly on ground
  Pressed are his footsteps in triumph of speed.

Stop they not once to refresh from the heat;
  Stop they not once to drink waters so blest;
Guided are horses, that seem to compete,
  On to the passes so rough in the West.

Fainter and fainter are clatters so hurried
  Heard from the distance,—they wane more and
      more,—
Gone altogether,—in silence deep buried.
  Vast is the mystery for horsemen before!

THE ARMY OF LIFE.

LIFE is a march to pinnacle afar,
Robed in a glare like a beautiful star;
Viewed is it often, by fancy's strong sight,
Gay in the day and as gay in the night.
Great is the Army of Life on the plain,
Formed to advance to its wonderful reign,
Loud, to inspire, as bold music is blown;
Loud as stern chieftains their orders make known.
Onward they move with strange banners on high,
Anxious, like mortals belated, to vie,
Bright as Phœbus is far pouring the ray
Shadows to cast of their forms on the way.
Happy are many with hopes in their breasts,
Proudly they step and erect are their crests;
Others are wan, yet ambitiously go,
Vain to appear as though free from all woe;

But hard the task for soldiers who are weary,
Feebly to tread with expressions so dreary.
High in the distance, as barriers to will,
Ridges and peaks, which are voiceless and still,
Rocky and bare, are now standing in wait
Once and forever to cripple each gait.

THE LAMENT.

The barren time of Winter dull and drear
   About on earth hath laid a snowy veil;
And northern winds are in the atmosphere,
   That with a slow but constant pow'r assail.

The sun is shrouded by a cloud on high;
   A shadow's cast upon the frozen plain;
A quiet melancholy hovers by
   To hold the noon a vassal to its reign.

Icicles shake and break and fall to ground,
   Appearing as they lie like gems of price;
Yon brook is mantled o'er, it gives no sound,—
   Its tide is rolling 'neath a sheet of ice.

Where late, on either side, the hedges bore
　　Among the thorns the golden-colored dower,
Is shrivelled all, for aged Autumn hoar
　　Came wrinkled forth and touched with fatal
　　　　power.

As down the lane with wand'ring course and
　　　　slow
　　The humble feet tread on the rugged ground
No plants on swelling banks with beauty glow
　　To spread perfume upon the breeze around.

Yet farther on, where trees of forest rise,
　　There's desolation still for eyes to trace,
As startled from a lofty bough now flies
　　A bittern to some far familiar place.

The ebon crow perched on yon oak-tree grim,
　　With ruffled feathers, must now pensive feel
As chilly trembles go through every limb;
　　But a complaint his tongue will not reveal.

Now hark! a woodman wields an axe alone,
 And strangely comes the distant muffled blow;
Then next the crashing trunk is heard to groan,
 And prostrate lies before a human foe.

As on the pilgrim roams with mood forlorn,
 The rabbits ramble in dim paths to go;
And through the solitude of woods are borne
 Fluttering leaves long warped and blown and
  low.

Yet he was wont soft other scenes to view:
 What time the hums prevailed in day serene,
When May came brightly clad to boons renew,
 To gladden Nature with a merry mien,

He walked at early dawn, then scorning rest;
 His frequent form observed the dewy bloom,
The bird industrious o'er its little nest,
 The vales and hills the gradual green resume.

To aid then friendship its influence gave:
  Ah, friend no more!—departed to a bourn
Which each must go—the lonely church-yard
      grave—
  To slumber long until arise last morn.

We were the happy tenants of the shade;
  Oft hearken'd to the mingled murmurs both;
Espied the blossom in the scented glade
  Thriving at root of some majestic growth.

As wisdom ruled the chamber of the brain,
  Gravely he talked of mankind's good and ill;
In future deemed would bend earth's evil reign
  Obedient to time's conquering will.

With faithful zeal upon life's daily course
  Small duties were his labor to perform;
To noblest thoughts that are of holy source
  His gentle spirit made the man conform.

When hard misfortune came with baleful train,
　Many dark periods passed, but never a tone
Fell from his lips to utter word of pain;
　He deemed it penance to endure alone.

When summoned from this world, resigned to fate
　With senses calm, he yearned no more to stay;
And, as a hero with the good deeds great,
　Chose for his chief the Lord of gentle sway.

Farewell, true friend! sober yet cheerful heart!
　Desires perceive no others such as you.
In place of what's denied, O Time! impart
　Congenial day to better moods renew.

Though when the Spring returns he'll not be here
　To breathe the air refreshing, pure, and mild.
But why lament? 'Tis vain to shed a tear
　Wandering on by solemn thoughts beguiled.

Even the Winter has its pleasant view;
  For it, like earthly life, prepares the mind
To relish richer gifts beyond—adieu
  Sad thoughts! and lead no more; ye are pur-
    blind.

THE PROMISED LAND.

WHAT gentle realm of truth now haps are o'er!
  Despite of weary ways we've reached this
    goal.
Old trials, vexations, and pangs no more,
  'Tis sweet to think, will perturbate the soul.

In day beauteous scenes far spread lure the view
  As blooming plants perfume a healthy dale;
The couch of slumber grants, at twilight dew,
  Tranquil repose, no mournful dreams prevail.

Heav'n seems to give content whilst breathing
    here
  From allurements—farewell, ye baneful store!
Leaving those things impure, once idols dear,
  Was hard, but harder now to them adore.

We can with wisdom's mood behold the past :
    How little are the means of trouble, toil,
When are indifferent eyes upon them cast,
    Knowing again they'll never us embroil!

The river's breadth, the sandy waste and wild,
    Great rugged crags upon the mountain high,
Were tasks, alas! to o'ercome as beguiled
    The fancy to this far and pleasant sky.

The Winter's cold, as Boreas thrilled the air
    When struggling slowly on the frozen plain;
The Summer's fervent heat or lightning glare
    Our movements to deter prevailed in vain.

When melancholy ruled the gloomy hour
    A faith benign sustained the spirit low;
Rewards foretold and some eventual pow'r,
    And urged the steps to calmly onward go.

Yet the numbers are great in distant rear
  Who daily journey to this quiet spot;
The thoughts, perhaps, within their minds are
      drear,
  Saying they vainly toil for what is not.

May each one persevere through daunts around,
  Essay at length to gain his deep desire,
And from the weight he carries be unbound
  When settled in a realm of truth entire!

THE TWO THOUGHTS.

Two thoughts arise: asks one a sacrifice,
　A pilgrimage most weary to the feet;
The other grants enjoyments to entice,
　Assuaging ease and golden apples sweet.

The tempter tells of troublous doubts away
　Like little winged plagues by winds far borne,
Arcadian raptures in luxurious day,
　Mellow slumber and dreams from eve till
　　morn.

Then longs the heart at times to throw the
　　weight
Imposed by Duty, scorn her humble mien,
Walk in the specious paths foredoomed by Fate
　To mar all virtue with eventual teen.

But it, mistrusting, views the wish with fear,
   Redeems itself from distant dangers known ;
And then resolves again to persevere,
   Encounter tasks sustained by faith alone.

Sustained by faith that tells of meeds at last
   To cheer the spirit when life's storm is fled,—
When rains from the dark clouds no more are
      cast
   Upon the wanderer's devoted head.

Then go for aye, thou tempter of the brain !
   Thou evil guest who barters for the soul ! ·
Thy credit, wealth, and tales alike are vain
   To lure to what will prove a gloomy goal.

We pledge our vow to thee, O Duty grave !
   In robe of sombre hue like hermits wear,
Ne'er leave thy rugged road, but on to brave
   As half-clad soldiers hoping whilst they bear ;

Nor think of things unmeet in false array,
　But rather them behold unstripped of powers,
When they the forms of noxious weeds betray
　That feigned to be amiss enchanting flowers.

A DAY-DREAM.

'Tis sweet to possess a do-nothing hour
　To muse on themes most absent from the time;
Then let the thought, in this lone Summer bow'r
　Within the garden gay, conceive and rhyme;
Be borne far back to some enchanted dale
Where wonders quaint and magic tints prevail.

No dreary spot it is to wander in
　Where giants grim, who live in guilty state,
Are wont to be away from worldly din
　And captives make of lonely men that late
Get lost within the limits of their reign;
When seized, alack! there evermore remain:

But a bright spot that has a charm to thrill
　And encourage the human soul forlorn;

4

That keeps dull-eyed Despair, against his will,
　Within a cavern's gloom to sit and scorn;
Wherein a Sybarite might choose to roam,
Leaving the city's throng 'neath pleasure's dome.

The winding paths and copse-clad slopes are
　　rife,
　The rocky grottos and secluded nooks;
And where, in valley's bed, with busy life,
　The bee can murmur near the crystal brooks
To cull the honey from the wild rose flower,
As gleams the sun with calm, methodic power.

Upon the ground are seen the pheasants rare;
　And floats about the easy butterfly;
The humming-birds are eager in the air;
　The deer browse in a grove of oak-trees nigh,
Where each expanded tree shows a leafy mass,
As though striving its neighbor to surpass.

But lo! behold on sward a figure rough;
　He wears upon his head a cap of green;

About his loins a robe of leather tough;
  The sandals brown upon his feet are seen;
Within his hand a bugle bright is held,
From, with his breath, harsh notes just now are
    swelled.

The echoes through the devious ways rebound
  Pygmean shouts.   From hidden depths wee
      men
And women odd before continued sound
  Made by the lusty blower assemble, when
Some turn to chat; these wrestle, run with
      glee;
Those test their skill at nimble archery.

Within a moving chariot comes their queen;
  Vanguards on steeds herald approach apace;
Behind numerous maids, enrobed in sheen,
  On small palfreys borne, praise in song her
      grace;
But ah! the poet's art cannot prevail
To vocalize their clear melodious tale.

Anon they stop before a bowery throne;
  The mild-eyed queen steps forth with graceful
      air,
And mounts its pleasant shade to sit alone,
  Whilst all the glittering train surround her
      there.
She's come to reign and see what pleasures gay
Amuse her subjects till tired close of day.

O dale! thy store of joy allures the view;
  Pleases with temptation the hopeful mind;
Invites, beneath a cloudless breadth of blue,
  To far-off goal which pilgrims cannot find:
What haps befall, with Fancy arch to guide,
If any sought thee in all the world so wide!

THE RIVAL SINGERS.

A PHANTASM.

A FAIR maiden in song ('twould wake a lyre)
   Outpoured her sweets upon the morn about
   From casement high, as Echo seemed to shout
In accordance; and both combined a choir
That pleased the ear, revived the inward fire.
   A single bird upon a tree without
   Was strangely charmed, his thoughts in utter
      doubt,
For knew he was outsung; but then to like
      aspire
   Required his throat new notes to strongly
      strain
Upon the air. Then the maiden his store

Outdid with better art.　But once again
His tongue perforced a lay to amply pour
　A reckless flight of sound.　Alas, in vain!
His blood he burst and fell and died in pain.

THE DREAM-GARDEN.

OF some old goal, by waxen light,
I read one eve ere Autumn blight,
Till mental heat conveyed me where
Were strange objects and wonders rare.
Then next I read sonorous lines
In Virgil's book; beheld green vines,
Fair trees where golden fruit was found,
Meads where crystal brooks rolled around;
And deemed I heard a simple swain
Inspire a reed with rustic pain,
Suggesting by his idle way
A rapturous do-nothing day.
Moved by dark hours, when low the head
Fell down to muse upon a bed,—
A lyre's soft buzz and far-off chants
Soon lulled my soul to slumber's trance.

Methought I roamed a garden wild
Where day-born radiance, breezes mild,
Numerous murmurs from the bees
Combined with beauty thoughts to please.
The umbrageous pathways were spread
Round hillocks streaked with blooming red;
Tender flowers and whitest buds
Outpoured perfumes in scenless floods.
The cool shades beneath purple grape
Served beds for beasts of savage shape,
But tame they were as purring cat
Dozing the morn on lazy mat.
Some pygmean monkeys were seen
Upon a banyan-tree with mien
Disportive; hard by nimbly swung
A parrot with a noisy tongue.
The white cygnet, the peacock vain,
The ostrich gay, the flying crane,
Divulged on high, on grass, on lake,
Their plumes and limbs of comely make.
I wandered on to southern side,
With reckless motion for a guide,

By grove of sturdy oaks where throngs
Of canary-birds chanted songs.

Observed was soon a cavern near;
Next snoring tones allured the ear;
As terror's charm a vigil kept
A giant large before it slept;
And made his clothes of leather tough,
And gnarled his face with vigor rough.

As I wandered still to behold
Varied scenery beyond unrolled,
Were heard anon a timbrel's sound,
A madrigal and tripping bound,
Implying sport upon the green
In some secluded sylvan scene.

Through copse I peered: within a glade
Afar were maids; beneath wide shade
They laughed and danced as a figure odd
(Holding a pipe and shepherd's rod)
Above them sat on limb of tree
To bid their steps move gracefully.

Elated he to see each go
Swiftly, skilfully to and fro;

And to assist the mazy bound
Inspired from pipe an unknown sound,
So purely sweet, to thrill so prone,
Ye might confess it a fairy tone.
At length he ceased, to ground leapt down,
With sudden motions turned to crown
A head with verdant wreath, next ran
Eagerly away like fabled Pan;
Far swelled his shouts in woods, as then
A calm came o'er the lowly glen.
The maids dispersed; some sought deep caves;
Others fair forms to river waves
Resigned, as Echo's sharpest mock
Prolonged their words from rock to rock.
   'Twas next I heard a cock's loud crow;
Startled from sleep I gazed, when lo!
The moon's gold beam was in the room
To color the carpet's pale bloom.

THE THREE POETS.

THREE poets once sat by a spring,
Whose waters bubbled up to sing,
As the warm sun was in the sky
With wealth of gleams to daze the eye;
Rough clouds of gray high overhead
Were slowly roaming shades to spread;
Upon the air, soothingly prone,
Was heard from bees a monotone;
And butterflies suggested life
Devoid of irksome worldly strife.
    These poets three conversed awhile,
Indolent moments to beguile;
And hope and life, pure love, dark death
Were of the speech they formed with breath;
And profound thought was oft combined
With graceful wit and fancy kind.

A charm prevailed in all was said
Like that in Nestor's words, which led,
As Homer says, the stubborn heart
To yield before their earnest art.

Upon the road a soldier bold,
Gallant and brilliant to behold,
Journeyed, and seeing bards on bank,
Begged for a draught, and of it drank;
Then talked of warfare, glory great,
Of deeds, of pomp, and kingly state;
And one of them enticed away
To go and be a warrior gay.

Anon there came a man more slow,—
A merchant he,—of coins which glow,
Rare gems, nice spice on far-off trees,
Where India breathes the odored breeze,
He discoursed. Another was lured
To seek where riches were secured,
To lay up comforts for old years
'Gainst poverty's long train of fears.

Next came a sailor of the sea
With awkward motions, accents free,

Who sang of merry days in life
On the blue deep when winds were rife.

He hailed the poet who, alone,
Was sitting, musing, on a stone;
But soon together o'er the hill
They roamed as friends at twilight still.

The years rolled by, but now no more
Are heard such tongues to amply pour
The varied phrases near the spring
Whose waters bubble up to sing.
Yet of those men no tidings tell
What haps to each in time befell;
And not a scroll upon the earth
Recounts all traits that formed their worth.

AN ALLEGORICAL DREAM.

I DREAMED I walked a palace hall
Whose pillars were both strong and tall;
Long I wander'd from side to side
Beguiled like one in Paradise;
Beheld the gauds of beauty mute,
The builder's skill, the painter's fruit,
The sculptor's statue, whose white art
Vied not from Nature to depart;
Listened to murmurs mildly float
Through the high aisles from parts remote;—
When lo! beside a brazen door
Garnished with figures o'er and o'er,
Erect and bold, scarce breath she drew,
A matron stern allured the view,
Who, like tragic queen on the stage,
Essayed to muffle inward rage.

A passion wild was in her vein
Like eagle's heart among the slain,
As though she would ever defy
All foes with menace in her eye.
Her robe was of a sable shade;
A crown on head; a dagger blade
Upheld one hand with firmest grip
Like cord a sail to shiv'ring ship;
And oft she waved it in the air
As bidding phantom fiend beware.

Anon there flew a winsome dove
(Sweet emblem it of gentle love)
Through an arched window opened wide,
Its feathers with faint purple dyed.
About it roamed with happy mien
As here and far 'twas often seen;
And then, a strength fatigued to rest,
It settled on the matron's breast,
When lo! from grasp the dagger steel
Fell to the floor to ring and reel;
Then spread like magic on her face
Emotions such as charm and grace;

The arm no more expressed a will
To deal a blow—peacefully still
It was.　Soon she glided away
Light in spirit as a lamb in May,
Caressing with many a word
The innocent and timid bird.
Unheard was then the murmurs low;
I wondered why, and turned to go,
When the dream-fancies of repose
Suddenly came to a wakeful close.

THE FLUTE.

———

As solemn darkness settles down
Upon the quiet village town,
The ticking clock against the wall
Breaks silence in the cottage hall,
But not a· word is heard to greet,
But not a clatter in the street,
But not an echo in the drear
To startle once the atmosphere.
Hard by the window where the vine
Spreads odors from the blossoms fine,
I idly sit and muse alone
And list from far the flute's low tone.
What anxious wight its form inspires?
And is he sad with vexed desires
Thus to the hour a mood make known
With a slow-born and tender tone?

Perhaps he plays to Daphne dear
Across the cornfield's bearded sphere,
Waiting like Juliet all forlorn
To see kind Romeo ere the morn.
The sounds seem to give sigh for sigh
That Summer breathes through oak-trees nigh;
Purifies the spirit with a sense
That music only makes intense.
Calm bliss it were fore'er remain
With pure emotions now that reign;
A king might yearn for such a state,
And bid world-grief be doomed by Fate.
Alack! they must attain an end,
Themselves with Time's wide distance blend;
Be only known as joys far flown,
Fond records of an evening lone.
But yon sweet flute, with Love's delay,
Pour forth thy note, if not for aye,
Until tired thoughts with slumber wed
And dream upon a soothing bed;
Peace may continue in the night
And bring dream-music to delight.

DORUS.

THERE is a maiden lovely to the view,
With winsome ways and eyes of spying blue,
Called Dorus (after a mourned-for mother dead),
Whose cheeks are oft with modest blushes
    spread;
Withal her meekness beauty makes her known
Like some conspicuous star at night alone.
To see her rural charms gay suitors came
From distant parts, confessed the secret flame;
But to their pained hearts eager to employ
Soft melting tones she was a little coy,
Often denied access, retired to bower,
There mused and wished, yet dared not tell a
    flower
What swain inspired the strange, acute unquiet,
Startled her pulse to leap in soul-like riot.

So odd is Love that scarce its breast will tell
What new-born joy is coming there to dwell.

I deem to know which adorer she loves,—
'Tis me!   Ah, joy delicate as a dove's!
Although of it not certain is my mind,
Yet feigned conviction serves beguilement kind
Whilst roving this grove of melodious ease
To ponder in the shade and gentle breeze.
For Dorus dear I long with earnest heart;
I'll try to woo her with nice Cupid's art
From rivals proud,—try that ideal to be
Which mildly forms within her revery.
When mine I'll take her to some happy seat,
Of which the poets write in cantos sweet,
That's found away from cold North's dreary
        sphere
In Southern climes where temp'rate months
        appear.
At morn we'll hail the fruitful vineyard bright,
The dew-bathed orange swinging in the light,
The shady palm, the aloe of the dale,
The fragrant myrtle and mimosa frail;

In calm accord with bliss gracing the day
Roam here and there to observe beauty gay;
List the simple shepherd begin to sing,
List the winding valleys their echoes ring.
Then we shall have noons sequestered, tranquil,
Reading in books romances at our will
Of barons bold and ladies of degree
Who lived in castles great with dignity.
At eve we'll sit in a solitary bower,
Hear the brief ditties of a mellow power,
The tinkling instruments of minstrels nigh
Wand'ring to soothe beneath a star-lit sky.
What joys, which yearners long to last for aye,
Could they be ours to charm our married way!
But ah! Dorus may not be mine to bless;
Some swain may woo her heart and cause dis-
      tress,
Leave me an object of Love's scorn to rove
And lament to the trees within this grove,
Like a lonesome bird without a mate to care
Whether or not he labors with despair.

A VAGARY.

———

THE pats of rain, so softly light,
Are heard on roof of house to-night;
They seem to be of spirit kin,
And lull my thoughts to peace within.

The groves at morn and fields at eve
They bid me rove health to retrieve;
But woman's love is better far
Than whistling bird or golden star.

Though Love will go to mossy dells;
He has his freaks and transient spells:
The sun more bright, the sky more blue,
Another sphere he seems to view.

The cygnet's grace upon the flood,
The beauty native in the bud,
A form that's shaped without a flaw
Are hers by mystic maiden law.

Rare colors the fresh bouquet twines
With odors sweet and verdant vines;
Rare virtues that make pure the heart
Ennoble her with lack of art.

The cottage window's little gleam
Spreads twilight rays across the stream;
And all about seemed holy air,
For nothing fatal hover'd there.

'Twas her abode hard by we met
Upon the plain where dews were set,
As the keen moon with golden arms
Enwrapped her form with added charms.

But sound the clangs,—within the hall
The clock knocks ten with brazen ball;
And all is still within the rooms
As all is still within the tombs.

Now Sleep come near to bring me dreams;
My couch is soft; and Darkness seems
Beside to droop as pats are light
Of rain on roof of house to-night.

MAUD.

THE moon shines on the bedroom floor,
  The clock ticks in the hall,
A shadow that's against the door
  Seems a dreary midnight pall.

Upon the bed, both white and meek,
  She seems a breather low;
But ah! the cold upon her cheeks
  Forbids to think it so.

No passion now in mortal vein;
  The pain of life is o'er;
The spirit to a dread domain
  Has gone for evermore.

O Maud! how canst thou slumber there?
   Thy lover's at thy feet;
Thou wert not 'customed to forbear
   With glance his glance to meet.

But yet he cannot, cannot deem
   Thee otherwhere for aye;
To conquer sorrow is to seem
   Thee back some future day.

THE QUERY.

Now come, my love, this early hour,
  Let us from cottage sally,
Go down the path and pluck the flow'r
  With odored-sprinkled face;
  And then with easy pace
Wander to leafy willow of the valley.

We'll stray through mead with dews ablaze,
  And as the lambkins dally
Upon the slope with winsome ways,
  We'll talk of days serene,
  And then of Cupid keen;
Yet seek the leafy willow of the valley.

Beneath the shade we'll sit and see
  The brook go clearly gliding,

As buds the banks o'erbend to be
  Reflected in the tide,
  As bees with busy pride
Seek the honey in their sweet depths abiding.

We'll watch wee fishes in their sphere,
  Enrobed in sparkles neatly,
Go here and there, conceiving fear
  As some bold danger nigh
  Swims with an eager eye
In search of dainty diet tasting sweetly.

Wilt be a fish, my love? I'll be
  A net; from foes that frighten
With cordage strong e'er surround thee;
  And in our lifely stream
  We'll float in peaceful dream
To sea of age where golden stars enlighten.

THE TRAVELLING FOX.

A TALE.

In bygone times (unknown the date exact)
There lived a fox upon a fertile tract
In parts remote.   Abundance gratified
Hunger, and fearful snares were unespied.
Now this young fox, that was safe from alarm,
Desired, alack! to go afar to view
Lowest-born vice and better manners new.
Although the world was blemished with disgrace,
Yet was distinguished for virtues of his race;
All the appliances of wiles to yield
Renown upon life's emulative field,
And many things besides to tempt the mind
Ambitious to excel were easy there to find.

Now this vain fox, with experience of life
Meagre, was bid remain at home when rife
Were entreaties to gain his sire's consent
To roam afar, though good was his intent:
To make new wit appear more bright than old;
To change all awkward ways from brass to
    gold;
In short, to make himself a perfect man
Before rivals,—a gallant gentleman!
But such folly displeased his father poor,
Who had known what things arose to allure
The youths to evil pits when he was young;
And who discoursed of them with mild forbear-
    ing tongue.
  Vexed at advice, the son resolved in spite
Of opposition to assume the right
Of departing from natal home away.
One Summer night, after tedious delay,
He stole from 'neath the sheltering roof alone
With quiet tread as swelled the snoring tone
From those in slumber low. Upon the plain
Was seen the moon above with stellar train;

But to the pale crescent or to starlight
He no attention paid. With a keen sight
He pursued a devious path, nor sought a rest
In nook sequestered for laboring breast.
Indeed, how saving he was then of time!
Exultation arose to think was prime
His body's health as now the world before
Allured. Soon various visions came to store
His mind with hopeful thoughts; they promised things
   things
In future days from which enjoyment springs.
 He reached a deep mysterious woods where trees
   trees
Were thickly set; and where the voiceless breeze
Failed to turn the limb's leaf,—it was so still
'Twould bear a whisper recesses to thrill.
Soon he lost his way. Thorns beset about
As fruitlessly he searched to get without
The lonesome limits wide. Anon a roar
Was heard; from lion stern it came that bore
Upon the path to thicket where he lay.
Alas! knew not this frightened fox which way

To turn for safety as perplexed he saw
Devouring danger boldly nearer draw;
But all his strength within, as trembles spread,
He summoned up and made a leap and fled,
As followed in the rear the object of his dread.
Through dark solitudes the fox scud with will,
Attained a plain, strived to attain a hill
From whose deep sides were delved gray quarry-
    rocks,
Chiselled and trimmed into large building-blocks:
He quickly glanced among high piles to find
A secret nook, but failed, left them behind,
And sought, with force fatigued and panting
    breath,
A furnace far with door of narrow breadth,
Where fires within were kindled to make lime
By neighboring peasants from time to time;
But as it chanced when gained, good luck for
    him,
There were no flames to burn the woody limb.
Secure he was from midnight beastly wrath
That raved for prey upon the winding path.

The lion soon came up and saw through door
The safety of the fox, observed him o'er
Awhile, and snuffed the air as though to say,
" Escaped, have you?" then growled and went
    away.
  Now fled the time till sparkling hours of morn
Came softly on the landscape to adorn;
Then Reynard peered to find if way was clear
Of dangers all, with eyes of timid fear.
The glorious sky had its vast blue unrolled,
The dew on grass·was brilliant to behold,
The gentle birds upon the trees sang praise
To Goodness great who reigns unseen always.
Anon, afar, some peasant men he viewed,
Who slowly walked and joked with manners
    rude;
Shovels were in their hands; a cart and horse
Behind them were, with boy to guide their
    course;
And before all rollicked about two dogs,
Which leapt up high, then rolled on ground like
    logs.

Reynard's heart beat most quickly in his breast;
Numerous troubles began to invest.
He moved from mouth of door. to darkest
　　part
Of the furnace.　Rumbles of the slow cart
Were heard to mingle with the gibes of
　　men.
He strongly hoped they'd pass his hiding den
And dreadful dogs not know a foeman there.
Nearer they moved!　Poor Reynard would not
　　dare
Stir just then, or across the plain to flee;
This act unwise might very fatal be.
Approached all slowly, noisily more near;
Most every nerve seemed list'ning in his ear!
Such sense was in his anxious mind to thrill
As half deprived him of surmising will.
They stopped before the door; next the dull
　　sound
Of falling tools and wood from cart on ground
Was heard; a master voice what things to do
Ordered, as feet about the furnace drew.

Soon gnarled branches of wood were thrust
    through door.
They meant to build a fire!   To ponder more
Was vain!   Resolved he was without delay
To up and leap and wildly dash away;
With a strong active spring through door he
    went,
By startled men his onward motion bent,
Who soon threw stones to stun his eager flight,
Which failed to serve aright each thrower's
    sleight.
The dogs deigned the meanderings to trace,
But cunning skill defied their baying chase.
   Reynard attained in time a thicket drear,
Where shadows screened from view.   Here he,
    as near
A crystal brook flowed by with a silvery tune,
Calmly reposed until the hour of noon;
Then he softly crept from lurking-place to go
Upon his journey, still resolved, though low
His spirits were, onward to travel far,
For wilful he when dangers did debar.

Now just it is to praise this fox so young
For great courage with words from truthful
      tongue.
A weaker heart would have returned in shame
To home; recounted to friend, with nervous
      frame,
Of daunts which him opposed upon the way;
And for forgiveness to parents he'd pray.
Not so for him!—return and hear the jeers?
Oh, no! he'd wander on a score of years
Amid life's perils all, afar from home,
Before he'd steal to friends from harm afraid to
      roam !
    The lack of food he felt as on he went;
Upon the soil he failed to find a scent
Which promised game, although he saw before
A rabbit swift that soon was seen no more.
    Up hill and down, and through a valley green,
Over a brook where fallen tree was seen
Above the tide, that served from bank to bank
      a bridge,
Up the high mountain to the crumbling ridge,

Next down through woods and on the public road,
With feelings in his mind which ill forebode,
He took his lonely, weary route, nor beast
He saw, till twilight dull was in the East.
   Full tired, he jogged along with moistened
      tongue
Extending from his mouth as breathed his lung
So hard, for great was now the evening heat
Upon the road where traced his dusty feet.
Hard by, on either side, tall trees uprose
With branches dark; and then succeeded those
The rough ascents, whose rocks were pierced
      with caves;
Such where Melancholy the time enslaves
With dismal pow'rs, and where the bat and owl
Are wont to live, and where the jackals prowl.
But mystery which seemed to reign within
This sombre place, did not repel, but win
His steps with prudent motion slow, to gain,
As urged his need, a morsel for his pain.
Just then he heard a noise as from despair,
And thought some timid thing in cave was there,

Too far it was beyond in dark to tell

What beastly form was 'customed there to
    dwell.

Again he list awhile; more loud the sigh

Was borne upon the air. He went to pry

With ears erect. A meal to eat was near!

He stretched to see if aught it was to fear,

Yet windings hid from view. Ah, felt he sure

Of food! no hunger longer he'd endure,

But go within, and there his stomach feed

With tender bits so nice and much as he did need.

He hadn't proceeded far with cautious air

And wily eye, when lo! around to dare

With looks a band of youthful wild-cats stood,

Their actions strange which meant for him no
    good.

Ah! vexed he was to think with art they'd
    caught

A fox whose tricks were better than they
    taught.

Superior sense inspired his breast amain

With noble pluck; he felt for them disdain;

Plebeians he considered them beneath,
And soon to flight he'd put them with his
    teeth.

The wrathful onset soon commenced; around,
At every point, they sieged on vantage-ground,
And on the single fox in fury fell
With snarls and sounds which nothing there
    could quell.
In his rough flanks they buried deep the fangs,
Which made sore wounds to cause the after-
    pangs;
But still with courage true he held the field,
Nor ever thought nor ever tried to yield;
And some of them compelled to hie from sight
As sudden cries bespoke their painful plight.
In time the wild-cats fierce, with waning strength,
Suspended blows to tire him down at length;
And they secure at distance viewed him o'er,
Re-licked their limbs where trickling was the
    gore.
Now it became the fox to make attack,
Or else a prisoner stay. They forced him back

When saw the foe he made attempts to leave
The winding cave, and step by step retrieve
Liberty; yet this act but angered him
Indeed, the more, and quiver'd every limb
As at antagonists he rushed in hate,
Resolved to wrest from them the purposed fate
They had in store for him,—a sudden death,
With not a friend near by as fled his vanquished
    breath.
Then dreadful confusion prevailed awhile:
The scuffling feet and snarling tongues, the pile
Of wounded venting loud the frequent howl,
As screeched above the scene the doleful owl;
Scudded gray rats from nooks with eyes of
    fear,
And ran about to wildly disappear.
Alas! Echo afar, within her aerial sphere,
If she an effort made, could not have mocked
The mingled tones of woe that swelled and
    shocked:
Nor meet it is for pen to here recite
What all befell the sanguine hour. The might

Prevailed at last, because a courage true
Inspired until a conquest was in view.
It is a mark of a craven heart to quail
Before the petty things which it assail.
Alack! 'tis so,—much freedom's gained in life
By hearts engaged to test themselves in strife.

Beneath the moon the victor fox now went;
His limbs were sore and stained, his strength
was spent.
He longed for rest, soon found a refuge lone
To lay him down to sleep; there with a moan
Long thought, alas! of home and quiet bed
Where he was wont to lie with weary head;
And in his fancy saw a mother dear
Who came to soothe his pain when he was sick
and drear.

When morning came to mantle with her light,
Awoke each beast and fowl from gloom of night.
The fox arose to startle in the way
A hare, which food supplied without delay.
What vigor filled his body! Humble food
How rich, inspiring thou, however rude,

When hunger wanes the bosom's strength! O
　　fox!
Thy joy was great as gormandized thy chops.
Often didst thou muse o'er, in future days,
That lucky meal which helped thy hope to
　　raise.
　Without adventure worthy here to write
The fox roamed on for days; now sad, now light,
His spirits were.　The various scenes beheld
Beguiled ofttimes and anxiety dispelled.
One noontide he observed, with gladsome eye,
A cultured valley wide, when corn and rye,
Tall wheat and clover red were tilled on soil
By yeomen strong inured to daily toil;
In fields innocent sheep with tinkling bells
About their necks; upon green hilly swells
Lowing cows; farther off the lofty height
Of a barn, as then he heard with quick delight
The crow of cock.　Transport was in his breast!
It was the place for him to live at rest
And life enjoy!　Just then came up to him
Another fox, and graceful was his limb.

"Ah, brother dear," said he, "where speedest
  thou ?"
To this query he answered, with a bow,—
An awkward bow,—he roved the world to see,
Its manners note, rare knowledge learn, to be
A polished gentleman. Then the twain fell
Into a long conversation to tell
Of this and that, at end of which they went
Within a woods where leafy bushes bent
About the entrance to a hidden cell,
Where beasts more large in comfort warm might
  dwell.
  Numerous things for appetite around
Within were strown like those that oft abound
In rich men's larders. Beds, of feathers brown,
And meet for head that's mantled with a
  crown,
Were spread upon the ground, where, every
  hour,
Slumber allured. Low, in a drowsy pow'r,
With lazy eyelids, lay the forms most sleek
Of foxes five. Ah! simple truth to speak,

They were fat rogues. They on the stranger
    cast
Uncivil looks, but welcomed him at last
When he of grace who brought the trav'ller
    there
Had winked, unseen by him, with jaunty air;
For they designed to make of him a dupe.
Ah, where the manners proud that will not
    stoop
From dignity to let a servant in
Who comes to pander to a selfish sin?
  In a week the stranger fox was more at ease;
They all grew kind about and deigned to please.
His lot was novel; it ne'er knew such time!
What fellows these, and just within their prime!
What tales were told! What midnight liberty!
All snares of men were known to them; and
    free
Themselves they could, if caught in same, so
    well.
They dwelt in a merry world and nothing ill
    befell.

Pillage was their labor with full content
At night whilst stars illumination lent.
Their wary ken and scent they nicely plied,
Which evil traps and cruel dogs defied.
Though the stranger fox was consigned to woe
When he was rudely forced to come and go
At superior command, or oft to do
An act of theft as his masters to view
Were near, secure for flight; yet choler sped
When he and they around the feast were
    spread.

  Yet bliss is like a crystal river swift,—
More speed more soon to taint with mud its
    drift;
It flows and from itself a brightness sends,
Then, ah! in time, with darkness deep it blends.

  One cloudy day appeared within the cave
A fox from foreign parts. His mien was grave;
His age was old; limped a lame foot, an eye
Was blind, but he saw keenly objects nigh
With the other one. He remarked alone
He came, to all of the company unknown,

Yet pardon begged, not meaning to intrude.

He wished to favor them, and to allude

To circumstances of great import indeed,

As he had heard of news demanding heed.

He continued: I was hid in a brier

Hard by some men in a field, who worked for
    hire;

I heard them say it was their purpose soon—

Perhaps to-morrow was the day, at noon—

To dig into this cell, its inmates kill,

And then again with rocks the opening fill;

For farmers could no more withstand the pest

Which roamed the land when they were gone
    to rest.

The rogues received this news with deep dis-
    may;

Frail fear was in their glances to betray

The workings of their minds. Sweet mirth to
    gloom

Was turned, so late in wide beautiful bloom!

With numerous anxieties oppressed,

Regrets arose that they must leave a nest

Which was so snug, in exile thence to roam,

Denied, perhaps, the pleasures of a home.

As each made haste to forsake the abode,

Dull night was near, great clouds were high, the road

Was dark. The stranger urged them forth; and told,

With mild, deluding tongue, where from the cold

And wet of storm portending in the sky

They could a shelter find both safe and dry.

Behind far trees they soon were gone from sight;

Then the old cunning fox in great delight

Glisten'd his single eye, for pleased his heart

To see the foolish dupes away depart,

And leave him master of the ground about.

O craft supreme with none ill words to doubt!

Anon he trotted off in easy style,

Retired beyond a hill more than a mile,

Returned again, and with him had a crowd

Of jolly foxes prime with aptest arts endowed.

Then of the cell the knaves possession took
With sly gratification in each look.

   As sped the fugitives on devious ways
With anxious hearts, on high began to blaze
Swift lightning; sounds of thunder rolled along
The moving clouds; broke leafy branches strong
As winds arose beneath the rumbling sky;
Trembled the earth, or seemed to tremble, nigh;
Thick darkness nestled on the ground; no form
Could be perceived as burst the fatal storm,
And on their heads came down the rain and
     hail;
And terror filled their breasts and caused them
     low to quail
They scattered were, strayed like lost sheep about,
Nor knew what objects near. Some sought in
     doubt
To find the cell; others to it returned
With frightened thoughts, but to be harshly
     spurned
Away by usurpers within. No grace
Had they to counteract their knavery base;

Nor sympathy for dupes so full of pain,
Standing benumbed in fury of the rain.
Then these deceived foxes, alas too late!
Learned they were decoyed by a tale—a bait—
To lure them from the comforts of their life;
And all was lost without defensive strife.

When daylight early came the clouds on
high
Dispersed, opened to view an azure sky;
Then sparkled keenly on abounding green
Myriads of rain-drops to adorn the scene.
But whither went the trav'lling fox?—to share
What fate? He was alone, not knowing where
Comrades had gone. Pitiful sight! Forlorn
His eye; his hair had been by brambles torn;
Each flank by mud was stained. Conscious dis-
grace
Expressed the settled feature of his face.
Upon a hill he stood. No covert nigh
To rest and hide whilst on the day moved by!
With observation new he saw the East:
There was a busy town; which, for poor beast

Like him, no mercy knew.   To West he gazed:
A river rolled whose tide was roughly raised;
To brave its force — ah, fatal stream! — he'd
    drown,
Nothing near would prevent expiring bound.
To South, within a field were grazing sheep;
Hard by a shepherd boy did vigil keep,
Who whistled easy tunes, devoid of care;
But to go by the flock, with stealthy air,
Would danger lure, for dogs were often near,
Although they were not seen yet eager was his
    fear.
To distant North a level scenery spread
Like prairie vast; no lofty tree-tops shed
Refreshing shadows to allure soft ease,
But greenest grass was ruffled by the breeze
Around a tented camp with guns aglow;
Where stalked erectly soldiers to and fro,
As bold as Mars when ready for the blow.
  On objects all about now Phœbus shone
With tender gleams, and distant things were
    known;

Yea, the rare hues on varied land and sky
Could be discerned, though far, by searching
    eye.
This cautious fox opined a venture ill
At such a time to seek, off from the hill,
A safer place. Indeed, he would not go!
Conceived that wisdom wins with patience slow.
Ah, patient would he be, and lurk till night,
And hence would steal in gloom with careful
    sight!
  Low lay the fox in musing mood on ground;
The grass and plantain weeds arose around
And partly hid his form; beside him flew
The butterfly and bee, which stopped and drew
Sweet honey from the tops of clover red,
That here and there in patches small was spread.
'Twas then his mind a train of hopes conceived,
Which entertained him long. Oh, he believed
They all to pass would come in future days,
Assist himself above the rest to raise!
Experience had commenced to make him large;
Far views of life were his; and to discharge

His former self as one who was unwise
From mem'ry's praise he would, although with
    sighs.
In truth, what bits of facts he had acquired!
The various traps the various tricks required;
He knew them all by heart,—every device
Of man to seize he'd foil it in a trice.
'He thought awhile of sire, of mother rare
At home afar; and of domestic fare,
Which was not suited to a palate keen
That had enjoyed good food as yet to them unseen;
But he, perhaps, would be above their state,
Then they might hear with gladness of his fate.
Anon employed his mind, away to get,
A stratagem; a plan at once he set,—
Between the camp and tide soft steps he'd ply
At night whilst men are wont in sleep to lie.

    How Hope contrives a route to miss the bar
Where Fate presides and seeming dangers are!
But yet the very path we think is right
Oft haps to be the one for our despite.
It is an easy thing results to see

Before they're formed in time's futurity;
They always please like colors of the air,
Which nearer viewed the less of them are there;
And then, again, what fancies of the mind
The longer sought the less of them we find!

At twilight time down sank the orb of day,
Then mantled o'er were fields with sober gray;
And, after many weary waiting hours,
The fox thought free to creep by herbs and
    flow'rs,
Onward to pass the tents. The river rolled
Upon the jagged rocks with dashes bold;
He feared its force, but was obliged to go
Upon the bank beneath chance shadows low,
Security to seek in distant parts.
He neared the camp and stopped with nervous
    starts.
Beneath the kettles black were smould'ring fires,
Whose smoke sailed up as high as steeple
    spires;
As the pale moon above shone down to gleam
A cannon large was glancing like a stream;

There walked the guards about in pomp and
     pride,
Each silent as a ghost. Oft flapped aside
The canvas loose of tents as stirred the breeze;
Within, 'neath candle glares, in reckless ease,
Were forms at dice and cards; in others slept
Soldiers on straws and blankets on them kept.
The fox prowled onward; eager was his ear
For all the hazards strange that might appear.
Suspense was great, when lo! upon his track
Before him marched a squad. He must steal
     back,
And turned. Another squad! Between the
     two
He was as they approached. What must he
     do?
Hard by the path a chest with open lid
He spied, and leaped at once within and hid
By crouching low. Ah! grateful was his mind
To think a screening-place was near to find!
He heard afar the marching sound of men,
Desired to rise and watch them with his ken;

But dare not then, for they might see through
    gloom
And quickly come with vengeance for a doom.
But on they moved, now near! and nearer yet!
He slyly peeped above; his sight was set
Upon two faces gazing down on him.
Then swelled loud laughs and fell to quake his
    limb
The oaken lid. In dark he was alone;
Oh, lost fore'er! and plaintive was his tone.
He scratched and gnawed and fled around in
    fright,
But ah! availed they not against ensnaring
    might.
  Alas, poor fox! what woes are in thy breast
As low thou liest now in languid rest
With pensive eye! Is this the better fate
That was to come to elevate thy state?
A cage they made; it holds thee all day long,
And then all night thy sorrows to prolong.
With bayonets men come at times to prick
Thy tender sides, or with a limber stick

Annoy as near they stand to gaze and taunt,
Whilst timid fear is in thy mind to haunt.
Oh, pity might prevail to let thee go,
Or else prevail to not abuse thee so!
But 'tis most like thou wilt no more be free,
And death at length must end thy misery.

THE END.